Kerri Berry Lynn

Sonya Ballantyne
Illustrated by Celeste Sutherland

FriesenPress

Suite 300 - 990 Fort St
Victoria, BC, V8V 3K2
Canada

www.friesenpress.com

Illustrator: Celeste Sutherland
Editor: Sage

Funded with the Support of the Winnipeg Arts Council.
The Cree used in this book is the dialect spoken by the
Misipawistik people of Northern Manitoba. Pronunciation
will differ from region to region. Thanks to Bruce Ballantyne
and Chelsea Vowel

ISBN
978-1-5255-3875-9 (Hardcover)
978-1-5255-3876-6 (Paperback)
978-1-5255-3877-3 (eBook)

1. JUVENILE FICTION, READERS, BEGINNER

Distributed to the trade by The Ingram Book Company

Dedication

Sonya Ballantyne — Dedicated to Ellen George, my chapan, who really had 20 (and more!) dogs and the real Kerri Berry Lynn, my baby sister, who could tame the wildest dog. Lots of love to Mom and Dad who always let us get a dog. And Jellybean, the best dog in the world and forever immortalized in this book as Têpakohp.

Celeste Sutherland — Dedicated to my mother and father for always believing I can do more with my art and my best friend, Alesta, for forcing me to sit down and finish illustrating this book.

Kerri 'Kerri Berry Lynn' Ballantyne — I would like to thank my sister, Sonya Ballantyne and our friend, Celeste Sutherland for writing and illustrating a story from my childhood; our chapan for having the same love for dogs; our parents and grandparents for never saying no to me getting a new puppy; and to Sean, who has been a huge support system and started my love for Shiba Inus, I love you. I hope you all enjoy this book!

Cree Dictionary

Misipawistik (pronounced "Mist-a-pie-stick"): a Swampy Cree community located in Northern Manitoba on the Number 6 highway. Misipawistik means "Big Rapids" in Cree.

Chemawawin (pronounced "Cheam (like steam)-a-wa-win"): a Swampy Cree community on Cedar Lake located near Misipawistik. Chemawawin is a Cree word that describes fishing from two canoes with a net being pulled between them.

Chapan (pronounced "Chap-pan"): Refers to a great-grandfather/grandmother (used for both genders)

Peyak (pronounced "Pay-ak"): one

Nîso (pronounced "Nee-so"): two

Nisto (pronounced "Nees-toe"): three

Nêwo (pronounced "Nay-o"): four

Niyânan (pronounced "Nee-yan-an"): five

Nikotwâsik (pronounced "Nee-ko-tay-stik"): six

Têpakohp (prounced "Tep-a-cop"): seven

Ayinnew (pronounced "A-nye-nayo"): eight.

Awas (pronounced "A-wus"): a Cree word that means "get away". Often yelled at dogs that try to steal food from the table.

Atimwak (pronounced "A-tim-wak"): "Dogs"

Atim (pronounced "A-tim"): "Dog"

Kerri
Berry Lynn

is a four-year-old girl from

Misipawistik.

She has always wanted a big family: her small family has her mum, her dad, and her chapan.

Her chapan lives in Chemawawin, which is across Cedar Lake from Misipawistik.

Kerri Berry Lynn visits her chapan a lot.

Chapan has also wanted a big family. Chapan has

80 DOGS!

Some dogs are big, some dogs are small,
and others are in between.

Chapan's dogs rush to say "hello"
to Kerri Berry Lynn when she visits.

They hit her in a big wave of fur and drool.

Chapan loves two things:
Kerri Berry Lynn and her dogs.

Chapan warns Kerry Berry Lynn of feral dogs
that aren't as good or brave as her dogs.

They bite and hurt people and good dogs.

To protect her, Chapan gives Kerri Berry Lynn
a puppy until she has seven of her very own.

First is Peyak, the oldest
and the big sister of the dogs.

She is the leader of the other dogs:
Nîso, Nisto, Nêwo, Niyânan, Nikotwâsik,
and Têpakohp.

The seven dogs don't look the same but
they are all family.

They look after Kerri Berry Lynn
like big brothers and sisters.

Kerri Berry Lynn starts digging holes with her dogs.
She rolls around with them. And she tries to eat
from a bowl on the floor like the dogs!

Her mum puts her bowl back on the table.

Peyak gets her own bowl between her teeth and
puts it on the table; the rest of the dogs follow.

Mum Sighs

but lets the dogs sit at the table.

Kerri Berry Lynn is sad to be told her dog sisters and brothers will not be able to go to school with her.

But Dad and Mum tell Kerri Berry Lynn how important school is for little girls.

Peyak licks

Kerri Berry Lynn's face.

Peyak and the rest of the family will be at home when Kerri Berry Lynn returns.

The dogs are locked in the back yard while Kerri Berry is at school.

Mum notices the dogs moping around the yard with sad looks on their faces.

Even when Mum brings out their food, only Têpakohp, the youngest and the smallest, reacts. Têpakohp licks Mum's hand.

Nêwo is watching the road from the top of her dog house when she sees the school bus approaching.

She barks to the other dogs, and they jump to their paws in a happy frenzy.

Kerri Berry Lynn hops off the bus at the front of her driveway.

She holds drawings she did at school for her parents and for her dogs' houses.

A feral dog crosses the road and sees Kerri Berry Lynn walking towards the house.

The feral dog growls at Kerri Berry Lynn and skulks towards her.

Kerri Berry Lynn sees the dog and stops walking because she is scared.

The feral dog is in between Kerry Berri Lynn and the house.

Peyak, Nîso, Nisto, Nêwo, Niyânan, Nikotwâsik, and Têpakohp sense something is wrong.

The biggest dogs form steps for the little ones to jump the fence.

Nikotwâsik and Têpakohp take turns jumping at the gate latch.

Nikotwâsik gets it open with a snap of his teeth.

Kerri Berry Lynn remembers her chapan's words about feral dogs that bite and hurt people.

She makes a quiet scared sound but remembers Peyak and the other dogs.

Kerri Berry Lynn remembers her chapan telling her the dogs are good and brave.

Kerri Berry Lynn growls at the mean dog.

The pack rushes around the house and forms a circle around Kerri Berry Lynn.

Kerri Berry Lynn's growling stops.

She sees that the feral dog has a tight old collar around his neck.

He is skinny, his fur messy, and he looks hungry.

"Wait!" Kerri Berry Lynn says.

"I think he needs some food!" Kerri rushes to the back yard and to the dogs' houses.

Her pack keeps a circle around her.

Kerri Berry Lynn takes some left over dog food from Nîso's bowl and rushes back to the front.

Kerri Berry Lynn puts the food on the ground, and she and the pack back away.

The feral dog sniffs at the food and eats it. "See! He's ok! He's just hungry," Kerri tells Peyak and the others.

Peyak goes to the dog house and gets her water bowl and brings it back.

The feral dog that is not so mean happily drinks some water.

Mum sees the dogs helping the hungry one, and she tries to shoo them away, "Awas! That dog is bad, my girl!"

Kerri Berry shakes her head and walks over to him, out of her mum's reach.

"He's ok! He is just hungry and sad!" Kerri Berry puts the food down next to the hungry dog, and he yips gratefully.

He lets Kerri Berry

pet him.

The other dogs gather and make
sure the new dog is warm.

"I think his name is Ayinânew,
Mummy!" Kerri says.

Mum sighs, "Dad says you can't
have eight dogs though, my girl!"

Kerri Berry Lynn laughs, "I don't! I
have ayinânew atimwak!"

Mum helps Kerri Berry Lynn get
Ayinânew's old collar off.

They make
a space

for a new dog house in the yard.

Dad comes home and is going to call
Chapan to come and get her dog.

Kerri Berry Lynn tells Dad how
she saved Ayinânew.

Dad says, "Well ... maybe Chapan can keep him."

All the dogs and Kerri Berry Lynn look sad,
"But he needs us, Dad! We can be his family."

Dad smiles, "Well ... I guess he can stay."

The dogs rush Dad and give him kisses. Kerri Berry
hugs her dad and hugs Ayinânew.

Dad and Kerri Berry take Ayinânew to be checked out by the vet.

The vet is visiting Misipawistik
and is able to neuter Ayinânew.

He has to stay overnight
at the vet's mobile clinic.

The other dogs offer support
when Ayinânew comes home.

Dad makes a new dog house for Ayinânew and puts it next to the other dogs' houses.

Mum and Kerri Berry Lynn make sure there's many warm blankets and a nice new bowl of water inside.

Kerri Berry quickly draws another drawing for Ayinânew.

She puts one drawing into each dog's house.

That night, Kerri Berry Lynn and her 8 dogs all climb into bed with mum and dad.

Dad sighs and allows Peyak under the covers.

Têpakohp turns off the light.

Kerri Berry Lynn has her big family.

CPSIA information can be obtained
at www.ICGtesting.com
Printed in the USA
LVHW072254151118
597308LV00001B/1/P